Estelle Takes a Bath

Jill Esbaum

illustrated by

Mary Newell DePalma

Henry Holt and Company · New York

Henry Holt and Company, LLC, *Publishers since 1866*

175 Fifth Avenue, New York, New York 10010

www.henryholtchildrensbooks.com

Henry Holt® is a registered trademark of Henry Holt and Company, LLC.

Library of Congress Cataloging-in-Publication Data

Esbaum, Jill.

Estelle takes a bath / Jill Esbaum; illustrated by Mary Newell DePalma.—1st ed.

p.   cm.

Summary: Pandemonium results when a mouse sneaks into a warm kitchen

to escape a blizzard and startles Estelle in her bubble bath.

ISBN-13: 978-0-8050-7741-4 / ISBN-10: 0-8050-7741-3

[1. Baths—Fiction. 2. Mice—Fiction. 3. Stories in rhyme.] I. DePalma, Mary Newell, ill. II. Title.

PZ8.3.E818Est 2006   [E]—dc22   2005019751

First Edition—2006 / Designed by Amelia May Anderson

The artist used acrylic paint and mixed media to create the illustrations for this book.

Printed in the United States of America on acid-free paper. ∞

1 3 5 7 9 10 8 6 4 2

For my dad, who introduced me
to my favorite doctor, Dr. Seuss
—J. E.

For Nina and Olivia
—M. N. D.

This is Estelle, of Toadburger Grove,
sipping green tea in her tub by the stove,
ignoring a blizzard, forgetting her troubles,
sunk to her chinny in peppermint bubbles.

This is the shivering, snow-dusted mouse,
who Squeezed himself into Estelle's little house.
The candlelit kitchen was pleasantly cozy.
The mouse was relieved (and entirely too nosy).

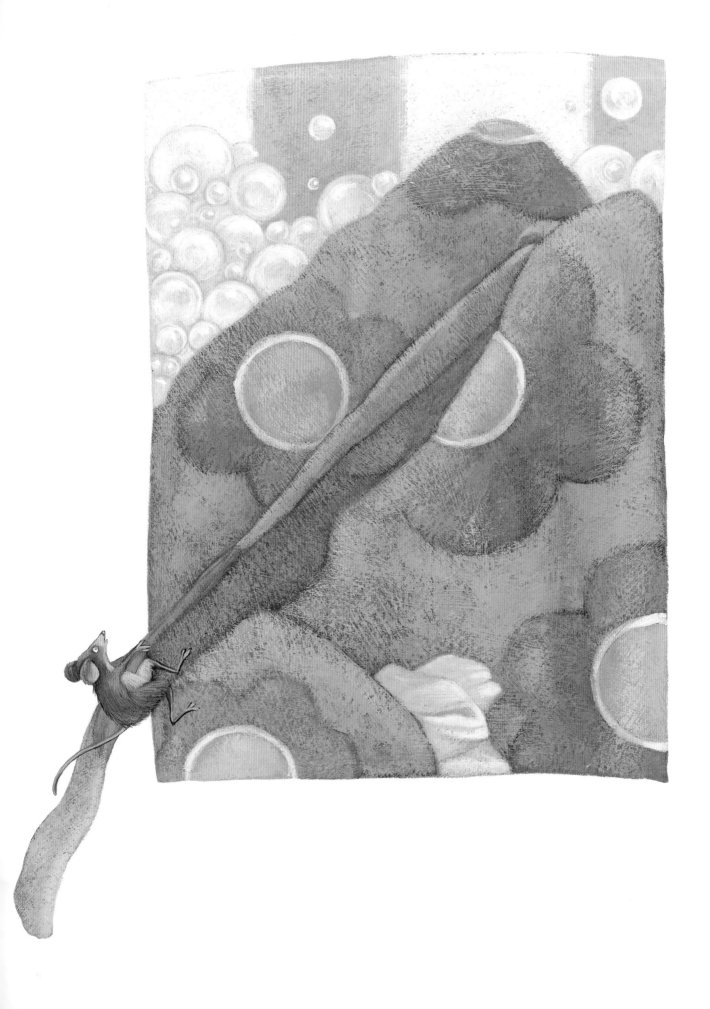

He climbed the old bathrobe tossed over a chair
to snuffle a noseful of peppermint air.
When kissers connected, bet no one could tell
just who was more startled—the mouse . . . or Estelle.

An earsplitting scream rocked the wee little house,
and an innocent visitor (namely, the mouse)
got an eyeful of heart-stopping, nightmarish stuff:
a volcano of suds and Estelle . . . in the buff.

She danced the Watusi and hollered some more

while bubbles splish-splattered all over the floor.

Her walloping heels stomped a thunderous beat (Estelle's not especially light on her feet).

The mouse skidded sideways, Estelle grabbed a broom,
and scritch-scratchy toenails *slip-slid* through the room.

There was **bumping**

and **thumping**

and **lurching**

and shrieking,

bouncing

and **hopping**

and suds-muffled squeaking.

She vaulted the table. He hurdled a shoe.
She slam-bammed the broom and took out the shampoo.
His life flashed before him; he cried for his mother.
Oh, **WHERE** was that exit? This way . . . or the other?

He leapfrogged the teakettle, scorching a foot, as the stovepipe exploded in sparkles and soot.

Her big toe got clobbered. His twitcher got nipped.
He still might have made it . . .

. . . except that he slipped.

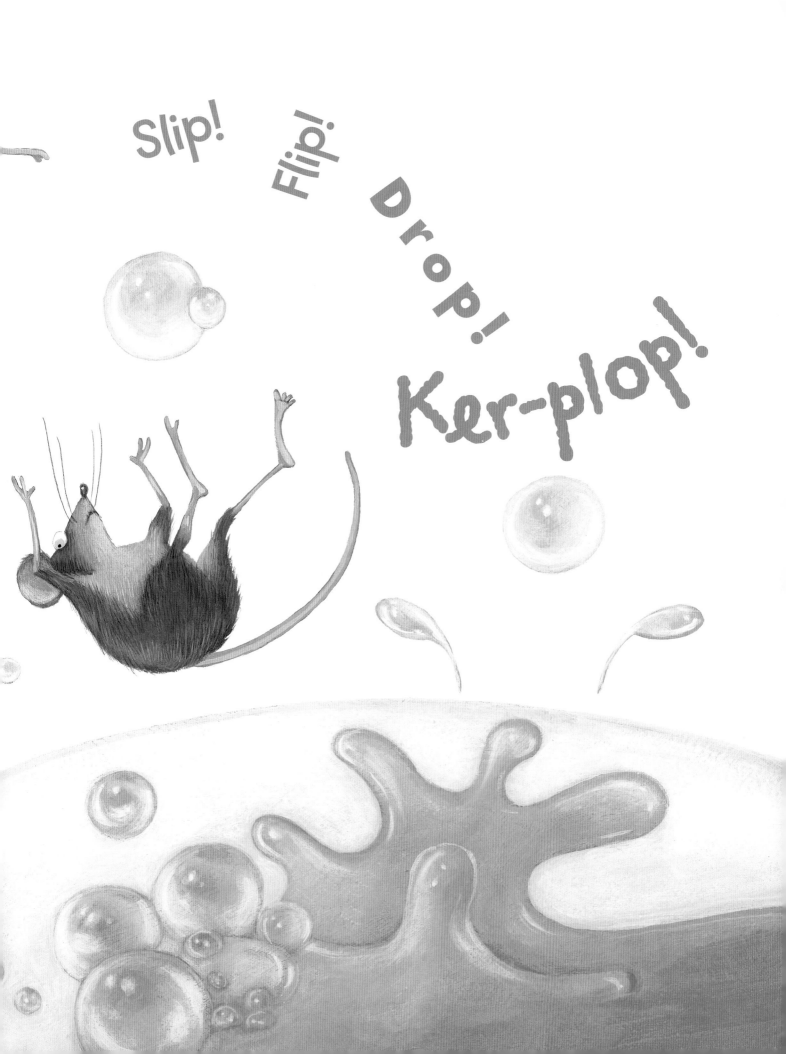

The mouse choked and spluttered and paddled and coughed,
and Estelle felt her mouse-hating heart going . . . soft?
She found herself suddenly frightened for him.
It was clear as her elbow: This mouse couldn't swim!

Despite her wrecked kitchen (and throbbing big toe), from deep in her belly Estelle bellowed,

"NO-O-O-O-O-O-O-O!"

Oh, who would have thunk it?
That mouse and Estelle
wound up sharing her kitchen . . .

. . . and bubbles, as well.